**A First Flight® Level Three Reader**

# Matthew and the Midnight Pirates

By Allen Morgan

Illustrated by
Michael Martchenko

Fitzhenry & Whiteside

First Flight® is a registered trademark of Fitzhenry & Whiteside.
Text copyright © 2005 by Allen Morgan
Illustrations copyright © 2005 by Michael Martchenko

Published in Canada by Fitzhenry & Whiteside,
195 Allstate Parkway, Markham, Ontario L3R 4T8

Published in the United States by Fitzhenry & Whiteside,
121 Harvard Avenue, Suite 2, Allston, Massachusetts 02134

www.fitzhenry.ca   godwit@fitzhenry.ca

10 9 8 7 6 5 4 3 2 1

**National Library of Canada Cataloguing in Publication**

Morgan, Allen, 1946-
Matthew and the midnight pirates / by Allen Morgan; illustrated by Michael Martchenko.

(A first flight level 3 reader)
ISBN 1-55041-902-1 (bound)–ISBN 1-55041-904-8 (pbk.)

I. Martchenko, Michael  II. Title.  III. Series: First flight reader.

PS8576.O642M29 2004    jC813'.54    C2004-900444-1


**U.S. Publisher Cataloging-in-Publication Data**
(Library of Congress Standards)

Morgan, Allen.
Matthew and the Midnight Pirates / Allen Morgan ;
illustrated by Micheal Martchenko.
Originally published as Matthew and the midnight pirates; Toronto: Stoddart, 1998.
[40] p. : col. ill. ; cm. (A first flight: level 3 reader)
Summary: After reading about pirates Matthew decides to become one.
At midnight when a bus full of pirates stops in front of his house
he joins in on their adventures, and encounters a crew of midnight librarians.
ISBN 1-55041-901-1
ISBN 1-55041-904-8  (pbk.)
1. Pirates – Fiction – Juvenile literature.
2. Librarians – Fiction – Juvenile literature.  I. Martchenko , Michael.  I. Title.
[E] dc22   PZ7.M674Ma   2004

Fitzhenry & Whiteside acknowledges with thanks the Canada Council for the Arts,
the Government of Canada through the Book Publishing Industry Development Program
(BPIDP), and the Ontario Arts Council for their support of our publishing program.

Design by Wycliffe Smith Design Inc.
Printed in Hong Kong

*For Merlin*

*A.M.*

---

*To the newest member of the family,*
*Alexander Jacques Martin*

*M.M.*

## CHAPTER ONE

One day, when he came home from
school, Matthew decided to be a pirate.
He wanted to be the best one he could,
so he carefully studied a pirate book
he had borrowed from the library.

He made an eye patch and drew on a scar. He loaded his trusty water pistol and stashed his hoard of comic books under his bed. Then he hid lots of treasure all over the house: the tub plug, a clock, his mother's hairbrush, a pair of her earrings, and all of her socks.

He made some maps to show where everything was, then he hid the maps too because he knew a pirate could never be too careful.

When dinnertime came, Matthew looked down at his plate in dismay.

"A pirate would never eat grub like this. We have pizza and root beer and licorice."

"That may well be on other ships," his mother agreed. "But I'm Captain here as well as Cook, and the menu is mine to command."

Actually, dinner turned out okay. Matthew stuck his hand up his sleeve so his fork looked like a hook when he ate.

## Chapter Two

While Matthew was helping to clear the table, his mother turned on the radio news.

*The library budget is up for a vote. The librarians need more money to buy books. Are the ones you've borrowed overdue? You'd better check! If the meeting doesn't go well tonight, the librarians might have to raise the fine for books that are late.*

Matthew had a terrible feeling his pirate book was a bit past its time. But when he ran upstairs to check, he couldn't find the date due slip in the front of the book. He wasn't sure what he should do so he took the pirate book out to the porch and hid it under the welcome mat.

Later on it was time for a bath. Even though Matthew explained to his mother that pirates never took baths, she didn't agree.

After his bath Matthew had to return all the loot he had hidden. He never did find the earrings, though.

"I'll find them for you first thing tomorrow," Matthew said as he got into bed.

"I hope you do," his mother said. She kissed him goodnight and turned out the light. Matthew closed his eyes. Soon he was fast asleep.

## CHAPTER THREE

Matthew woke up at the stroke of midnight. He heard the sound of a horn outside, so he went to the window. A bus with a mast and a pirate flag was waiting on the street below.

Matthew put on his pirate gear and went outside. When he arrived, the bus door opened. A plank was lowered. Matthew grinned and stepped aboard.

15

The bus was full of midnight pirates and all of their pirate stuff.

"I always thought pirates sailed on the sea," Matthew said.

"We don't like water," the captain explained. "It makes great ammunition, though, so we keep some for our guns."

"What would a guy like me have to do to become a pirate like you?" Matthew asked.

"Not very much," the captain said. "We don't take baths and we never shave. That's about it, more or less."

When Matthew said he was just the same way, the pirates agreed that he could join their crew.

Suddenly the lookout cried, "Thar she blows! Pizza van off the starboard bow!"

"Go get him, me hearties!" the captain cried.

The pizza van tried to get away, but the pirate bus was much too fast and the chase didn't last very long.

The Midnight Pirates ransacked the van and carried away fifty jumbo pies to get them through the night. But before they could take a single bite, the lookout shouted again.

"Librarian bus coming hard astern!"

## Chapter Four

"Those comic books in the hold are way overdue," the captain said. "We've got to get out of here!"

They didn't get far. The midnight turkeys jumped out of hiding and blocked their way, armed to the beak with water balloons.

"Look out, they've got water!" the pirates cried. They tried to turn back, but the midnight librarians came up from behind and captured the whole pirate crew.

The midnight pirates were chained in a line and taken away to make good on their fine. The librarians walked them out on a plank above a big tank of hot, soapy water.

"Not the water!" the pirates all cried. "We'd rather eat spinach! We'd rather die."

"Pay your fine!" the librarians told them. "We need the money. Our budget is going to be cut tonight."

It looked pretty grim. Matthew had to think fast.

"If you let us go without getting wet, we'll sneak past the guards at the meeting tonight and vote for more money to buy books," he said.

The librarians thought it was worth a try, so they let the pirates go free to see what they could do. The turkeys decided to go along too, to be their secret weapon.

# Chapter Five

When the pirates arrived at city hall, security was very tight.

"No pirate buses allowed tonight," the parking guard said.

"Got any plans about how to sneak in?" the captain asked Matthew.

"We need a disguise," Matthew replied.

The pirates thought Matthew's plan was good, so they hijacked a busload of midnight lawyers.

The lawyers cried and threatened to sue, but the pirates didn't care. They took the lawyers' briefcases, and tied them up in their underwear.

"We'll need to smuggle the turkeys in," Matthew explained. So they stuffed them into the briefcases and headed for City Hall.

The disguises worked well. Matthew and the midnight pirates arrived at the meeting just in time to present their case.

"Books are important, books are fun. You can't cut the budget. We need more books," Matthew said. Then he gave a signal and the midnight pirates opened the briefcases.

## Chapter Six

The turkeys giggled and wiggled their bums. They ran everywhere as they sang this song:

> *Books are wonderful! Books are neat!*
> *They're fun to read and they're good*
>   *to eat.*
> *Put them on pizza or into a pie,*
> *Prop up a TV or swat down a fly,*
> *Stand on a pile when you can't reach*
>   *a hook.*
> *You can do lots of things with a*
>   *library book!*

When the vote was finally called, the turkeys all voted, some of them twice, and the library budget was saved.

The midnight librarians were very pleased. The pirates didn't have to pay the fine for their overdue comics. And when Matthew told them about the book he had hidden under his welcome mat, the librarians promised they'd bring him a new date due slip.

The midnight pirates drove Matthew home. "Be in our crew any night you like, so long as you haven't shaved or bathed," they called as they dropped him off.

Matthew agreed and waved goodbye. Then he went upstairs and got back into bed. Soon he was fast asleep.

## Chapter Seven

Matthew woke up the next morning at five. He ran downstairs and looked in the book underneath the front mat. His new date due slip was in the back. And that wasn't all! He discovered the map for the earrings there too! X marked a spot in the garden nearby.

So, after he added a few special touches to make the earrings look better, he wrapped them inside the morning paper and ran upstairs to tell his mother the news.

"Wake up, Mom. Look at this!" Matthew's mother slowly opened one eye and peered at the newspaper.

"Council keeps the library budget," she read. "That's very nice, dear. Now go back to bed."

"The turkeys voted, I did too," Matthew said, and he told her about all the fun that he'd had with the midnight pirates.

His mother was still a little confused. "You harpooned a pizza van?" she asked.

"It's pirate stuff, Mom. It's just what we do. But that's not the best part; the best part is this."

Matthew unfolded the newspaper. The earrings fell out onto the bed.

"What happened to them?" his mother said.

"I added some things. They're pirate earrings now," Matthew explained. "So you can come be a pirate too—as long as you don't take a bath or shave."

# Have you read Matthew's last midnight adventure?

# Don't miss these other great stories!

FIRST FLIGHT®

# FIRST FLIGHT READERS

**Featuring award-winning authors and illustrators and a fabulous cast of characters, First Flight readers introduce children to the joy of reading.**

Short stories with simple sentences and recognizable words for children eager to read. Ideal for sharing with your emergent reader.

High interest stories and language play for developing readers. Slightly longer sentences and words may require a little help.

More complex themes and plots for the independent reader. These stories have short chapters with lively illustrations on each page

Much longer chapters with black line illustrations interspersed throughout the book for confident, independent readers.